When You Look at Me, Will You Love Me?

By Patricia Ann Reed

To order additional copies of this book, contact:
Xlibris
844-714-8691
www.Xlibris.com
Orders@Xlibris.com

ISBN: Softcover   979-8-3694-2351-6
        EBook   979-8-3694-2350-9

Print information available on the last page

Rev. date: 05/31/2024

When You Look at Me, Will You Love Me?

Noah walks in and says,
"Don't tell me to go sit down.
Say hello to me.
Ask me how I am doing today."

Elijah walks in and says,
"Don't tell me to keep quiet.
Let me share my heart with you."

Sophia asks Mrs. Cloves,
"When you look at me,
will you love me?"

3

Don't look at all my weaknesses.

See the great person that I am.

Don't tell me that you don't think I'll have a good future.

Tell me that I am destined for greatness.

Don't keep passing me by
as the class helper.

Let me help you sometimes too.

6

When you look at me, will you love me?

Don't tell me I can't do anything right.
Tell me I can do anything if I really try.

Don't tell me to stop crying.

Ask me, "Are you ok?"

When you look at me,
will you love me?

Don't say, "Oh no, she's here."

Tell me you are glad to see me today.

11

You are making our future with the power of your words!

When you look at me,
will you love me?

13

"Come here my friends,"
says Mrs. Cloves.
"It's something
I need to
tell you all."

When I look at you all, I love you.

Your future will be great!
You're fearfully and wonderfully made!
You are smart!
You are strong!
You are valuable!
You are loved!

I love you all.

16

When I look at you, I love you.

Printed in the United States
by Baker & Taylor Publisher Services